It's five years since Ben Tennyson last transformed into aliens and fought crime with his cousin Gwen and their Grandpa Max.

Now 15 years old, Ben is once again forced to turn to the Omnitrix to help fight a new and more sinister threat – the HighBreed, DNAliens and the Forever Knights, who team up to take over the world.

The watch-like Omnitrix has re-programmed itself and has a complete set of ten, brand new alien choices for Ben to get to grips with. Helped by his cousin Gwen with her magical powers and Ben's former enemy, Kevin E. Levin, Ben is soon all set to go hero once again!

NOW READ ON . . .

MEET THE CHARACTERS

Ben Tennyson
Fun, kind and brave,
he's a superhero

Gwen Tennyson
She's Ben's cousin, and
has magical powers

Kevin E. Levin
One of the good guys,
with absorbing powers

ChromaStone
A living crystal, almost
indestructible

Swampfire
Can shoot fire and
regenerate lost limbs

Jet Ray
Can fly, swim and has poisonous stingers

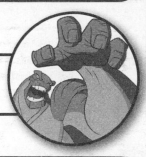

Humungousaur
He's huge and throws his weight around

Big Chill
A ghost who can become invisible

Paradox
He's a time-travelling scientist

DNAliens
Baddies, and loyal servants of the HighBreed

Manny and Helen
Aliens who seem to be after Ben's gang

EGMONT

We bring stories to life

First published in Great Britain 2009
by Egmont UK Limited
239 Kensington High Street,
London W8 6SA

Adapted by Barry Hutchison

ISBN 978 1 4052 5007 8

1 3 5 7 9 10 8 6 4 2

Printed and bound in Great Britain

The Forest Stewardship Council (FSC) is an international,
non-governmental organisation dedicated to promoting
responsible management of the world's forests. FSC operates
a system of forest certification and product labelling that
allows consumers to identify wood and wood-based products
from well managed forests.

For more information about Egmont's paper buying policy,
please visit www.egmont.co.uk/ethicalpublishing
For more information about the FSC, please visit their
website at www.fsc.org

PARADOX

+

PLUMBERS' HELPERS

PARADOX

CHAPTER ONE

THE ARMY BASE

In a top secret military base, a grey-haired army general was getting nervous. He was standing inside the observation booth of a laboratory, watching his two best scientists put the finishing touches to an experiment that could change the world. If everything went to plan then today – November 12th, 1955 – would go down in history.

If everything went according to plan. But the general's gut instinct told him something was going to go wrong, and those instincts had never failed him before.

He picked up the handset of the telephone he used to communicate with the main lab and barked into it. 'Sure this thing is gonna work?

Your time machine has cost the US government a pretty penny, doctor.'

The doctor leading the experiment gestured towards an enormous circle of stone and metal. It was mounted on a raised platform and filled most of the lab. Hundreds of wires and cables connected it to a control terminal.

'The Chronologger is hardly a time machine in the sense of a vehicle,' the scientist explained, 'but rather a subatomic drill designed to bore a tunnel in the fabric of space-time.' He turned to the glass screen, behind which the general was standing. 'As to cost, I would say that the alleviation of untold human suffering throughout history is ample justification.'

'It'll also give our enemies overseas a thing or two to think about,' the army commander grunted.

'But to answer your first question,' smiled the doctor, 'there is only one way to find out.'

On cue, everyone in the lab, including the

doctor and the general, pulled a pair of thick protective goggles over their eyes. Once he was sure everyone was covered up, the doctor crossed to the control terminal and pulled the activation lever.

SWOOOOSH!

Almost at once, the huge contraption began to shudder and shake. A wind whipped up from inside the ring, sending notes and books hurtling across the lab.

'You're certain we're safe, Doctor?' asked his assistant. He was standing a little further from the machine, monitoring the bank of energy readings.

'I'm not certain of anything, Hugo,' the doctor admitted. 'But the chrono-magnetic field we've created should protect us.'

Hugo wasn't convinced. 'Doctor,' he began, 'I . . . I'm frightened.'

The doctor rummaged in his pocket and pulled out a bag of sweets. 'Have a gumball,' he said, offering the bag to Hugo. 'It'll help calm your nerves.'

Suddenly, lights began to flash across the surface of the Chronologger. The howling wind became even more fierce. It swirled into a tornado and tore through the lab.

Hugo watched, helplessly, as the contents of the lab began shuddering across the floor towards the machine. He cried out in shock as a cabinet flipped into the air. It flipped end over end a few times, before being sucked into the time machine.

All around him, desks, chairs and bits of machinery were being pulled into the middle of the stone circle. Each one seemed to stretch out like rubber, then vanish through the hole in the heart of the machine.

Hugo glanced down at the energy readings. They were off the scale. He had to warn the doctor. The experiment had to be stopped!

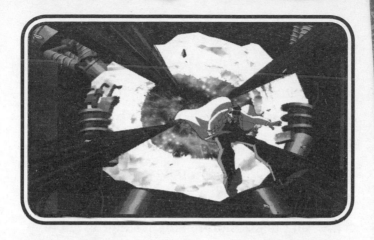

Before Hugo could say a word, the doctor began to slip. He swung his arms, trying to retreat backwards, but it was too late. His body became elastic, and with a strangled scream he was swallowed by the Chronologger.

A second later, a large shadow passed across the lab, and something the world had never seen before let out a deep, terrifying roar.

Kevin's car cruised along a narrow desert road, throwing up clouds of sand in its wake. The sun was beating down, making the three occupants of the vehicle hot and irritable.

'You didn't need to come,' Kevin muttered. 'Gwen and I could have handled this alone. It's nothing, really.'

'It doesn't sound like nothing,' said Ben from the back seat, as Kevin pulled the car over. 'Weird noises. Unearthly lights. Rumours of weird creatures out here.'

They threw open their doors and all three of them stepped out on to the dusty road. Before them stood the thick, imposing walls of a long-abandoned army base.

'Yeah, the dudes I heard it from aren't totally reliable,' Kevin admitted.

'Isn't that like a big bad boy thing to do?' asked Gwen with a smirk. 'Come out here to the ghost town to drag race?'

'How should I know? I just know them

from auto shop,' Kevin claimed.

'Grandpa Max said Las Solardad used to be a big military base back in the fifties,' said Ben. 'Some kind of research facility.'

Kevin nodded. 'Yeah. Must've been some pretty serious research. Check out these walls. Fifty years later and there's still no way in.'

Gwen gave a little cough. She had wandered away a little, and was standing beside two giant holes in the wall.

'No way,' Kevin frowned. 'They definitely didn't tell me about these.'

Gwen and Ben walked through one of the holes, while Kevin steered the car through another. Once they were all inside the base, Kevin got out of the car to join the others.

The base was laid out like a small town. Dozens of buildings lined a network of cracked, crumbling roads. Every one of the buildings was little more than a boarded-up ruin, long since abandoned.

From inside, it was possible to make out a few more holes in the walls of the base.

'Has anyone noticed that some of them are vaguely person-shaped?' asked Gwen.

Ben looked around at the holes. 'Weird,' he said. 'Maybe something, I don't know, burned through the wall.'

'Like what?' asked Kevin.

Ben pointed down to the ground, where a deep track had been carved through the tarmac surface of the road. 'The same thing that burned these weird trails everywhere.'

Gwen crouched down, examining something on the desert floor. 'Look,' she said.

Ben followed her gaze and soon spotted a tiny, perfectly-formed skeleton. 'This is a bird,' he said. Something at his feet caught his eye. He bent and carefully picked it up. 'And these are lizard bones. They're fossilized.'

Gwen straightened up. 'And they're not the only thing.'

One of the trenches in the ground led to an old telephone box. The box itself was a tangle of rusted metal, and two deep footprints were scorched into the stone floor, inside the telephone box.

'It's like someone turned the stone into dust just by standing on it,' said Gwen.

Kevin smirked. 'He was probably put on hold.'

Ben's eyes followed the route of the trench in the ground. 'The trail goes to the police station,' he announced. 'Then to those . . . I guess they're apartments.'

'So,' began Kevin, 'going by those fossils, someone stood here a million years ago and walked to those buildings that were built about fifty years ago?'

'You are not helping,' Ben sighed. 'These could be signs of serious DNAlien activity, and it's up to us – '

'DNAliens are not doing this,' said Gwen,

cutting him off. She raised a hand and pointed to where a weird, glowing-blue creature was snaking across the base. 'Does that look like a DNAlien to you?'

Ben had to admit that it didn't look like a DNAlien, but it did look dangerous. And he knew just how to deal with danger. The Omnitrix bleeped into life as he twisted the control dial.

It was butt-kicking time!

CHAPTER TWO

GROW UP, KEVIN

Kevin kept his eyes locked on the strange creature while he knelt down and pressed his fingers against the road, absorbing its energy. 'Finally,' he grinned, as his body began to turn to living concrete, 'something worth the trip.'

Gwen tensed, her fingertips glowing with power. Beside her, Ben slammed his hand down on the Omnitrix. A swirl of green energy wrapped around him. When it cleared, his alien form towered above his two companions.

'ChromaStone!' he cried, as the transformation into his indestructible alien form was completed.

And not a second too soon. The blue, snake-like creature swerved around the group and brushed against the side of one of the crumbling old buildings.

KEREEEAK!

The area that the thing had touched disintegrated into dust, and the whole building suddenly leaned sideways. ChromaStone looked up in time to see the entire structure toppling towards them.

'Look out,' he cried. He threw himself at Gwen and Kevin, wrapping his arms around them and dragging them out of harm's way.

CRAASH!

The building came down in a cloud of sand and sawdust. Sharp shards of the slate roof rained to the ground, missing the heroes by just millimetres.

ChromaStone leapt to his feet and spun in the direction the creature had gone. Another trench in the ground was the only sign that it had ever been there.

'Gone,' muttered the alien. In a flash of bright green he morphed back into Ben.

Gwen stood up and dusted herself down. 'Well, at least the building it destroyed wasn't the library.'

'You really like the books,' said Kevin, also transforming back into his normal form.

Ben sighed. 'She's saying we have to research. Find out what that thing is.' His eyes followed the criss-crossed tracks on the ground. 'All we know so far is that it's looking for something here on the base.'

Twenty minutes later, Gwen was sitting in front of an old-fashioned monitor, studying old microfilms of the base's research documents. It hadn't taken them long to find the library, but finding the information they needed was proving more difficult.

'These films are really corroded,' she complained, scrolling through another few pages of the documents. 'But it looks like this base was built for some kind of time experiment called "Project Paradox".'

Standing behind her, Kevin frowned. 'Who wouldn't pick the desert outside Bellwood to do top-secret research?'

'They built it here because of the huge quartz deposits,' Ben explained, reading from the screen.

Leaning over his cousin's shoulder, Ben

studied the photograph of a man on the screen.

'His name's been censored,' said Ben. 'Whoever he was, his paradox theory was the basis of some kind of experimental tunnel through time.'

Ben straightened up. If there were scientists carrying out research on the base, then that meant only one thing. Somewhere nearby there had to be a lab.

The laboratory was in even worse condition than the rest of the base. Moss grew over the stone walls and ceiling. The glass screen of the observation booth was cracked and broken. A deep trench ran the whole length of the floor, right up to the strange, circular object that stood on a raised platform at the far end of the lab.

'Looks like my place after that big party I threw last weekend,' observed Kevin.

Gwen pointed down at the groove carved into the stone floor. 'Look, that thing's been here, too.'

'Only one trail,' said Ben. 'It either came in here and vanished – '

'Or it was born here,' concluded Gwen.

A sound from behind startled them. Moving on instinct, Kevin absorbed the properties of the concrete floor. Ben's hand flew to the Omnitrix and pushed down the dial.

'Swampfire!' he roared, as he transformed into another of his alien forms. In a heartbeat he was through the door of the observation booth.

Something moved in the half-darkness. Pouncing, the alien caught hold of the shape and dragged it into the light.

'Gotcha!' he cried.

The face of the man they'd seen in the

photograph gazed up at Swampfire. The doctor smiled warmly, and as he did his eyes twinkled with friendly mischief.

'Swampfire. That takes me back,' he said, before his eyebrows folded into a frown. 'Or is it forward? It's so hard to tell, Ben. In fact, have we met?'

'How do you know my name?' demanded Swampfire, releasing his grip on the man's white lab coat.

'Have we met yet, I suppose the question was,' continued the scientist.

'Hey,' said Kevin. 'It's that dork from the photo. The paradox guy.'

'You haven't changed at all,' Gwen gasped. 'In fifty years.'

The doctor rummaged in his pocket and pulled out a crumpled paper bag. 'Oh, considerably more than that,' he smirked. 'Gumball?'

'No thanks,' said Swampfire, pushing the outstretched bag away. 'Who are you? What's your name?'

'You just read my file,' shrugged the doctor. 'I was rather hoping you could tell me. It slipped my mind several hundred years ago.'

'Did he just say "several hundred years"?' asked Kevin.

'Did you just say . . .' began Swampfire, before realising the man had vanished.

'By the way,' called a voice from behind them. The three heroes turned to find the doctor standing across the room. 'You didn't happen to see a space-time anomaly around here, did you?' He held up his hand to just above the level of his shoulder. 'About this big? Incredibly destructive, virtually unstoppable.'

The doctor waited for a reply, but none came. 'No? I must have been thinking of another moment,' he said with a shrug. 'Ta-ta.'

Turning on his heels, the doctor stepped through the door and left the lab. Kevin hurried after him, then stopped in the empty corridor.

'Where'd he go?'

Gwen pointed out of the window. The doctor was across the street, leaning casually on a rusted old street light. 'He's out there,' said Gwen.

'He's obviously connected to that creature,' said Swampfire. 'We really need to talk to him.'

'Oh yeah,' growled Kevin, cracking his concrete knuckles. 'We'll talk.'

With a roar, Kevin smashed a hole

through the wall of the lab. His stone feet thudded on the ground as he charged, fists raised, towards the scientist.

But with a wink and a nod of his head, the doctor stepped behind the narrow lamppost. And disappeared!

Kevin skidded to a stop, unable to believe what he'd just seen. 'Huh?'

From across another street, Kevin heard the sound of someone clearing their throat. The doctor stood in a doorway, waving happily. He stepped inside the building and closed the door as Kevin charged towards him.

KARAAACK!

The old wooden door shattered to splinters as concrete Kevin hurtled through it. Outside, Swampfire and Gwen watched the old building shake and tremble. Kevin was tearing it to pieces, searching for the doctor.

A footstep scuffed on the pavement behind them. 'Was I in there?' the doctor asked.

Grinning, he turned and ran around the outside of another building.

Swampfire and Gwen were quickly joined by Kevin. They blasted through the building, hoping to cut the doctor off before he could make it all the way round.

And when they emerged on the other side of the boarded-up house, the man was nowhere to be seen. They turned to find him standing behind them, leaning casually against the wall they had just destroyed.

'That was public property, you know?'

Swampfire shook his head. 'How does he move so fast?'

A voice from a little to their right surprised them. 'You mean how do I move so quickly?' corrected the doctor. He was across yet another street, even though none of them had even seen him move. 'It's called "walking",' he explained. 'Strolling, really.'

Kevin charged again, but this time the scientist didn't move. Kevin grabbed him by the lapels of his lab coat.

'Easy on the jacket, it's twelve hundred years old.' A twinkle danced behind the doctor's eyes. 'Anyway, thanks.'

'Thanks?' frowned Swampfire. 'For what exactly?'

'Well, I had a feeling if we made a loud enough racket he'd show up.' The doctor nodded along the street. The blue, snake-like creature was zig-zagging towards them.

'Finally,' growled Kevin, releasing his grip on the doctor. 'Something we can fight.'

'Oh, I really don't think that's a good idea,' the doctor warned, but it was too late. Kevin was already thundering towards the creature, his concrete hands clenched into fists.

'Those trails,' said Gwen, suddenly figuring everything out. 'They're not trail marks, they're age. The creature accelerates time.'

The doctor nodded. 'Very good.'

Kevin caught up with the weird blue snake and swung with a devastating punch.

The creature didn't even seem to notice the blow, which passed harmlessly through its glowing blue surface. Kevin, on the other hand, couldn't help but notice. The moment his fist made contact, his concrete shell vanished. Kevin let out a cry of shock as an agonising pain gripped his whole body. The others could only watch as he collapsed on to the road.

The doctor set off in pursuit of the

creature, leaving Swampfire and Gwen to tend to their fallen friend. They both recoiled in horror when they rolled him on to his back.

Kevin's skin was as wrinkled as a dried up leaf. His normally jet-black hair was wispy and grey, with a wide bald-spot on top of his head. Even his teeth had rotted away to nasty blunt yellow stumps.

It had taken only a few seconds, but somehow, just by touching the creature, Kevin had aged over eighty years!

CHAPTER THREE

RACE AGAINST TIME

Ben – now back in his human form – took hold of one of Kevin's arms, while Gwen took the other. Together they hauled him to his feet. 'We must get him to a hospital,' said Ben.

Suddenly, Kevin gave a cough and sprang into life. He pulled away from the cousins and raised his fists. 'What're you doing?' he wheezed. 'Get your hands off me.'

'Come on, Kevin,' pleaded Gwen. 'We're gonna get you some help.'

'What do you mean, "help"?' Kevin grimaced. 'I'm gonna kick that thing!' He swung a leg to demonstrate, then yelped as his hip made a loud cracking sound. 'Ow!' he spluttered, clutching his aching joints.

'Are you OK?' asked Gwen.

'My back's killing me, my legs ache, and what's up with these shoes?' Kevin scowled. 'Is it too much to ask for a little support?'

Gwen turned to Ben. 'He's like a real irritable, short-tempered, crotchety old man,' she whispered.

'In other words, aside from the male pattern baldness, he's pretty much the same as always,' said Ben, smirking. He started walking towards the car. 'Come on, old man.'

Kevin hobbled along behind, muttering below his breath. His frail fingers took the keys from his pocket and struggled to fit one into the door lock of his car.

'I'll drive,' said Ben, snatching the keys away from Kevin.

'Don't even think about it,' snapped Kevin. 'You don't have a licence.'

'Grandpa Max taught me,' replied Ben. 'And it's an emergency. You're near-sighted, arthritic, your reflexes are shot . . . and what's more, you're trying to unlock a cactus.'

Kevin creaked around and squinted his eyes. Sure enough, what he had thought to be the green paintwork of his car was actually a large, spiky cactus. He groaned. Maybe driving wasn't the best idea, after all.

The three heroes climbed into the vehicle, Kevin taking several minutes to clamber into the back seat. Ben slotted the keys into the ignition and the engine roared into life.

'You should have gone out with me when I was young and handsome,' Kevin told Gwen.

'You were too immature,' Gwen replied.

Kevin's eyes lit up, hopefully. 'What about now?'

'Too old.'

Before Kevin could respond, Ben floored the accelerator. The car lurched backwards and slammed into a large, metal, rubbish bin.

'Whoops!'

'It's not a bumper car,' Kevin snarled.

Up ahead, the front of a building exploded into dust. The blue creature snaked out from inside. It sped forwards, racing straight towards the car.

'Back up, back up!' cried Gwen.

Ben didn't need to be told twice. He pushed down hard on the accelerator pedal and the car launched into reverse again. His knuckles were white as he gripped on to the wheel, struggling to keep the car from spinning out of control.

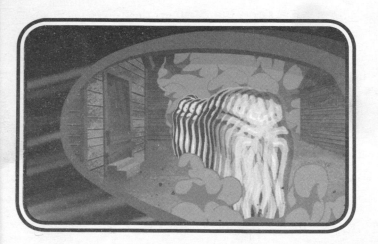

Glancing in the rear-view mirror, Ben could see that the creature was hurtling towards them. Slamming on the brakes and twisting the wheel, he sent the car into a slide. As the creature drew closer, Ben hit the gas again. The car lunged forwards into the mouth of a narrow alleyway, spewing up clouds of dust in its wake.

The ruins of the base's many buildings whizzed by on either side as Ben powered the car along the alley. He had his foot pressed hard against the floor, but it wasn't enough. The blue shape in the rear-view mirror was growing larger by the second.

And suddenly it was upon them. The creature's blue glow barely brushed against the outside of the car, but the effects were instant. The shiny green metal became brown and pitted with rust. Thick plumes of black smoke began to billow from the exhaust. Even the leather interior became worn and ripped.

'No, not the car,' wailed Kevin. 'Please, not the car!'

Even aged as it was, though, the spluttering engine still had some power left in it. The car erupted from the alleyway and skidded sharply to the right. A mound of old timber rested against a wall, forming a slope just a few hundred metres ahead. Ben steered towards it. If he could hit it just right . . .

'Hold on,' he cried, as the car sped towards the incline. He pushed even harder on the accelerator and closed his eyes, not daring to look. The car hit the makeshift ramp and launched into the air.

For a moment the three occupants of the vehicle felt weightless, before the car's tyres slammed down on to the flat roof of the building. The brakes squealed angrily as Ben kicked down on them. The car slid sideways for a few seconds, before coming to a rest right next to the edge of the roof.

They sat in silence for a few moments, waiting for their racing hearts to slow down. At last they slowly and carefully clambered out on to the roof.

'You are never driving my car again,' scowled Kevin.

'Where have you been? You were supposed to get here six seconds ago,' scolded the doctor. He was standing beside them on the rooftop, examining an old silver pocket-watch. 'Or is this thing running fast?'

'Who are you anyway?' quizzed Ben. 'What are you doing here?'

'What is that creature?' added Gwen.

'And can you fix my car?' Kevin asked.

The doctor looked at Kevin and stroked his chin, thoughtfully. 'There's something different. Is it your hair?'

'Yeah, I'm parting it down the middle now,' Kevin growled. 'And I also got real old.'

'Please don't talk to me about old,' smiled

the scientist. 'I walk in eternity.'

'Well you'd better start running in eternity, smart guy!'

'Hmm, you might slow us down. I need to fix that,' the doctor said, almost to himself. He gestured with a thumb to another corner of the roof. 'We'll come back right over there.'

Gwen and Ben turned and were amazed to see the doctor standing at the other end of the roof. Kevin was beside him, young and fit once again. Ben looked around, but the old man version of Kevin was nowhere to be seen.

Gwen hurried over and threw her arms around him. 'Kevin, I can't believe it!' she beamed. 'You're good as new!'

'Well, my back still hurts a little,' Kevin said. He rested his cheek against the top of Gwen's head. 'If I could just lean on you . . .'

Gwen stepped back and gave him a playful shove. Kevin smiled, then turned to face the doctor. 'All right, professor,' he said. 'If you wouldn't mind fixing my car.'

The doctor raised an eyebrow. 'How exactly do you expect me to do that? I'm a time traveller, not a mechanic. Regressing a car would break all the Chronal laws of space-time.'

'OK, enough,' snapped Ben. The way the doctor spoke was starting to make his head ache. 'I want answers. Now.'

'Same old Ben Tennyson,' said the doctor, smiling. 'You're even more like yourself now than you were in the future.'

Kevin shook his head and sighed. 'You want me to deal with him?'

'What can you tell us, Dr Paradox?' asked Gwen.

The scientist's eyes sparkled. 'Paradox. Oh yes, that'll do. That'll do very nicely. I'll tell you a story in a way you can understand, with a beginning, middle and end.' He smiled playfully and held out his watch. A blue glow rippled across its surface. 'We'll start in the middle.'

CHAPTER FOUR

A GLIMPSE OF THE FUTURE

With a blinding flash, the three friends found themselves seeing the events of fifty years ago through Paradox's eyes. They were suddenly inside the lab, working on the big circular object they'd discovered earlier. Another scientist stood nearby, nervously studying the readings on a control panel.

'Las Solardad was built entirely because of my ingenious theory,' the doctor's voice told them. 'A time tunnel utilising the properties I discovered in quartz crystals, which would allow us access to past and future events.'

An electric-blue light began to swirl inside the machine. Ben, Gwen and Kevin could actually feel the wind as it whipped up and scattered paper and notes across the lab.

'Yeah, well for a genius, looks like you blew it,' noted Kevin.

'You don't know the half of it,' replied Paradox, grimly. 'Some tiny miscalculation on my part destabilised the experiment and ripped a hole in the fabric of reality.'

The heroes almost cried out in fright as, through the doctor's eyes, they saw the swirling portal opening up to swallow them.

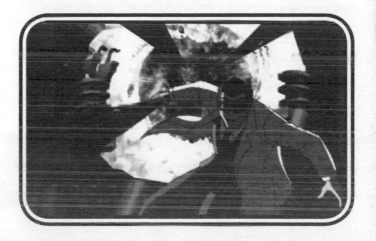

'I was hurled into the event horizon,' continued Paradox. 'I must have spent one hundred thousand years there. I didn't age or need to sleep or eat. I just existed.'

All around them, Ben and the others saw nothing but wide empty space stretching out in every direction.

'Heh. It must've been pretty boring,' Kevin said.

'At first I went quite mad, of course,' explained Paradox. 'But after a few millennia I got bored with that, too, and went sane. Very sane. I began to learn.'

With a flicker of light, Ben, Gwen and Kevin emerged from the flashback. They were back on the roof again, their legs shaking slightly from what they'd just experienced.

'I now have a total understanding of the space-time continuum,' Paradox told them. 'Allowing me to travel anywhere and in any time I want. Within reason.'

'And so where's your time machine?' asked Kevin.

'He doesn't have a time machine,' said Ben. 'He has a map in his head.'

'Exactly!' laughed the doctor. 'I know where all the shortcuts are. I spent a dozen lifetimes criss-crossing the time stream. Making it a better place.'

Kevin sneered. 'And how does that pay?'

'At the moment?' sighed Paradox. 'Not even in job satisfaction.'

The world seemed to go dim for just a fraction of a second, and all four of them were suddenly standing back in the ruins of the laboratory.

'You see, I recently discovered that some kind of extraterrestrial creature is going to wreak havoc across the universe.'

Ben frowned. 'So? The way you talk, you take on monsters like this all the time. Why's this one so bad?'

Snatching up a piece of chalk, Paradox began drawing a complicated series of scribbles on a blackboard. 'Because unlike the thousands of foes I've faced before, this extra-dimensional creature came into our plane of reality the moment my experiment went awry.'

'OK, so just to be clear,' said Kevin. 'It's your fault.'

'This creature hasn't been lurking around here for fifty years,' Gwen pointed out. 'We would know about it.'

'Time is like a river,' explained Paradox, chalking up a wavy line on the board. 'It moves, flows and bends. Fifty years ago, I accidentally set off a depth charge in that river. The creature I released was blasted fifty years in time to your present.' He scribbled all over the line on the board, wiping it out. 'Doing this to your future.'

'But all it's doing is messing up an old army base,' said Gwen. 'Why is that a problem at all? Why not just leave it alone?'

'That's a better question for the man on the moon,' chuckled Paradox.

'What?' asked Ben, confused. 'Who's the man on the moon?'

'I am,' grinned the doctor. He gestured around them at the barren, grey landscape, and twinkling stars.

Ben looked down at the dusty rocks beneath his feet. 'We're on the moon,' he said, matter-of-factly.

'No,' corrected Paradox. 'We're on the moon in your distant future.'

'What?' spluttered Kevin. 'How are we not suffocating?'

'Good question. Not remotely the point, though,' Paradox smirked. 'Imagine what the Earth would look like in two hundred years, say. With that time monster wandering all over it, aging everything that crossed its path.' He glanced at Kevin. 'For those of you with no imagination, the Earth is up there.'

They all looked up. Above their heads, a decayed planet orbited silently through space.

'You've brought us to the worst possible version of the future,' said Ben.

'No. Should I fail to stop that creature, this is your best possible future.' He waited a moment, letting his words sink in. 'Not a pretty sight, is it?'

A figure suddenly appeared a few metres ahead of them. It stood with its back to the group, gazing up at the shrivelled Earth.

'What are you doing here?' asked Paradox.

The newcomer turned around. It was the doctor. Or an identical version of him, at least. Kevin shook his head. This was frying his brain.

'I'm allowing myself to feel the full impact of my failure,' replied the other Paradox.

'OK,' sighed Kevin. 'Who's he?'

'He's a parallel Paradox,' Ben guessed.

'Young Ben has an innate sense of trans-temporal metaphysics,' the new doctor smiled. 'It will serve him well in his past.'

Ben grinned, pleased by the compliment, even if he didn't really understand it. 'And I drive good, too,' he added.

Kevin suddenly remembered the rusted old vehicle back on Earth. 'We can breathe on the moon in the future, but you can't fix my car?' he scowled.

'What should I do?' asked the first Paradox, ignoring him.

'Well, obviously not what I did,' shrugged the other. 'But whatever you do, you better do it quickly.' He turned his gaze back up to the lifeless husk of the planet Earth. 'Time is running out!'

CHAPTER FIVE

SOLVING THE MYSTERY

Reality flickered around them, and Ben, Gwen and Kevin found themselves back in the abandoned army base. Paradox was with them. Thankfully there was only one of him.

'So why do we come back here? Why don't we just travel back in time and stop the time experiment from ever happening?' suggested Gwen.

'Isn't that just like an energy being to think outside temporal conventions?' chuckled Paradox. 'The experiment that releases the creature also unsticks me in time. And that must happen, because, uh, in all modesty . . .'

'You've saved the world dozens of times,' concluded Ben.

'Hundreds, actually. In fact, on one

occasion you and I worked together to save the entire uni . . .' His voice trailed off and he shook his head. 'Never mind. It should be here any – '

KRAAK-OOOM!

The deafening roar of an explosion tore through the base. Paradox nodded. 'You could set your watch by it.'

Ben was setting his watch, but not in the way Paradox had meant. He adjusted the Omnitrix and scrolled through four or five of his alien forms. At last he found the one he was looking for.

'Jet Ray!' he cried, transforming into the red, winged alien. He launched himself into the air in time to see the blue creature emerge from one of the derelict buildings.

Jet Ray rained down a torrent of energy blasts on the monster. Each blast merely passed through the thing, not damaging it at all.

Paradox grabbed a handful of gumballs from the bag in his pocket. He hurled them at the ground just in front of the creature. It slipped and skidded a couple of times on the hard balls of coloured candy, then stopped.

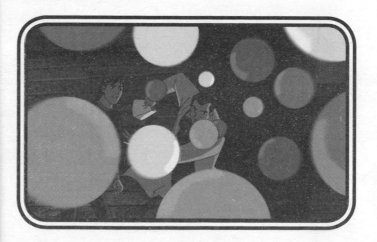

'They hit it?' asked a puzzled Jet Ray, touching down next to the group. 'Doesn't everything age into oblivion as soon as they touch it?'

'Gumballs last a really long time. Look under your desk at school,' Paradox replied. His eyes went wide with fright. 'Now get back!'

Jet Ray turned to see the creature speeding towards him. He kicked out with his powerful legs and flew out of its path at the very last moment.

Gwen raised her hands. Energy crackled across her fingertips, but before she could unleash an attack, Paradox threw himself into the creature's path. He caught hold of it and pushed, bravely trying to force it back.

'Let go,' Gwen cried. 'Or he'll age you into dust!'

'I exist outside of time,' replied Paradox through gritted teeth. 'But I can still feel the eons passing.'

Realising he was useless in his current form, Jet Ray flew down to land and changed back into Ben.

'Paradox, take us back to the accident,' he barked. 'Now!'

The doctor grunted. The effort of holding the creature back was draining all his strength. 'But I told you – '

'Just do it!'

One brief, blinding flash later, the heroes and the time-creature all found themselves back in 1955. Around them stood the same army base, only now it looked brand new.

'Kevin, Gwen, the lab, quick,' ordered Ben. He turned to Paradox. 'You just keep that thing occupied.'

'Keep . . . keep it occupied?' echoed the doctor. 'I'm a time-travelling hero. I don't keep things occupied!'

The door to the lab opened quietly, and Ben, Gwen and Kevin snuck inside. An imposing army general stood in front of a window, watching the experiment that was soon to take place on the other side of the glass.

'Sure this thing is gonna work?' the general barked into the handset of a telephone. 'Your time machine has cost the US government a pretty penny, doctor.'

Unseen by anyone, the three heroes crept out of the observation booth and into the main part of the lab. They crawled along the floor below the window, their eyes scanning the room for anything that might tell them how to stop the strange creature.

'As to cost,' said the doctor, continuing his conversation with the general, 'I would say that the alleviation of untold human suffering throughout history is ample justification.'

Down on the floor, a thought suddenly occurred to Ben. 'Why would it use the phone?' he whispered.

Gwen frowned. 'What?'

'The creature. It tried to use the payphone. Then it went to the police station. Then the dorms. It didn't act like some unfathomable trans-dimensional creature. It did everything a normal person would do.'

Gwen nodded, finally understanding. 'If they suddenly found themselves in an abandoned military base.'

With a roar, a wind whipped up around

them. The doctor had thrown the switch to start the machine!

They looked up in time to see Hugo, the lab assistant, accidentally knocking a heavy tool box on to a control panel. The machinery fizzled and spat as the circuitry inside went haywire.

The wind in the lab immediately increased in strength. Electricity buzzed across the surface of the time machine. The doctor stumbled forwards, and then he was tumbling across the lab. He cried out in terror as he was swallowed up by the swirling energy of the Chronologger.

'Help!' yelped another voice. Hugo was clinging tightly to a metal pole. His legs were dragged out behind him, toes pointing towards the machine. His knuckles were white. He couldn't hold on much longer.

Ben leapt up and stretched out a hand. As he did, he felt his own feet begin to slip on the rough concrete floor.

'You'll get sucked in along with him!' Gwen shrieked.

'I need to put on a little weight,' Ben realised. He slapped his hand down on to the Omnitrix and felt the energy swirling around him. The room shook as he stretched and grew into the hulking, dinosaur-like Humungousaur.

Shocked by the sudden appearance of the monstrous alien, Hugo let his fingers slip from the pole. For a split-second he was hurtling towards the Chronologger, before something brought him to an abrupt stop.

Hugo looked up to see an enormous hand gripping his arm. Humungousaur's mouth curved into a smile, revealing two rows of worryingly sharp teeth.

'Trust me,' said the dino-alien, 'this beats the alternative.'

With a grunt, Humungousaur pulled Hugo free of the swirling whirlwind. Energy flared at Gwen's fingertips, then crackled across

the room. In a flash of purple, the time machine
exploded, showering the lab with shards of
stone and hot metal.

Outside the lab, Paradox wrestled with
the time-creature. He was growing weaker. Any
second now his legs would give way and the
monster would be free to rampage across the
whole globe.

And then, without warning, the creature
stopped fighting. Paradox looked down to see
the semi-conscious form of his old assistant,
Hugo, where the monster had been.

'Hugo,' he said with a gasp. Suddenly it

all made perfect sense. 'Of course. If it were a snake it would have bit me.'

At the sound of their footsteps, Paradox turned to find Ben, Gwen and Kevin approaching. 'Well, don't look so smug,' he told them. 'I would have figured it out eventually.'

'You had a hundred thousand years,' Ben reminded him.

Paradox smiled. He released Hugo, who was slowly coming round, then stepped over to join his fellow heroes. In a flash of blue all four of them vanished, leaving behind one very confused lab assistant.

Back in the present, Paradox was preparing to say his goodbyes.

'Well, I have to admit it, I'm impressed,' he said. 'All those centuries trapped in the event horizon and it never occurred to me that the accident wasn't my fault.' He smiled at Ben. 'You're much smarter than you were when I met you years later.'

As Ben tried to figure out if that was a compliment or not, Gwen stepped forwards. 'And so what happened to him?' she asked. 'Your lab assistant?'

'I lived my life,' spoke a hoarse voice from behind her.

They all turned to see Hugo shuffling up to join them. He looked older than he'd looked when they'd last seen him. Fifty years older.

'Hugo,' beamed Paradox. 'How are you?'

'I'm well, and you look the same,' Hugo replied. 'And I haven't seen you in fifty years.'

'Well I haven't seen you in a hundred thousand years,' Paradox told him. 'And you don't look that bad. How was your life?'

'Good,' Hugo nodded. 'A good life. But, I'm . . . I'm sorry about the experiment. I ruined everything. I never got to time travel.'

Paradox raised an eyebrow. 'Would you still like to?'

'Yes. I'm not afraid any more.'

'Glad to hear it!' He put his arm around Hugo and began to lead him towards a swirling blue portal that had appeared just a few metres away. 'How about I give you a behind-the-scenes look at eternity?'

And with that, the two old friends stepped into the time portal, and vanished.

'Well, at least he's got company now,'

said Gwen. 'He won't be lonely any more.'

'Oh, and thanks for stranding us out here in the middle of nowhere,' Kevin shouted, even though Paradox wasn't around to hear him.

'Come on,' shrugged Ben. 'We've got a long walk home.'

The three of them trudged off towards one of the holes in the base's security wall. As they turned the first corner, Kevin's eyes went wide with wonder. His car sat in the middle of the road, its green paintwork gleaming.

'It looks like new,' gasped Gwen.

'It doesn't just look like new,' Kevin laughed. 'It's factory new from thirty years ago. Paradox, I take back everything I was about to say about you.'

A scrap of paper under one of the windscreen wipers caught Ben's eye. He picked it up, unfolded it and began to read.

'Kevin,' he read, 'try to keep in mind that if this car comes into contact with anything else from 1976, it will explode like anti-matter. Enjoy! Paradox.'

Ben folded the note and passed it to Kevin. 'He's kidding, right?' asked Kevin, the smile fading from his face.

Gwen and Ben climbed into the car, grinning to themselves.

'That's some kind of time-travel joke, right?' Kevin fretted. 'Isn't it? Guys?'

On the back seat, Ben gazed out at the army base. They had done it again. They had saved the world. And even though he may be a little strange, it was nice to know that someday, somehow, they would cross paths with Paradox again.

CHAPTER ONE

HELEN AND MANNY

Footsteps echoed through the empty halls of a locked-up sewerage plant, faster and faster, as if someone was running for their life. A man burst from the shadows, his eyes bulging as he glanced back over his shoulder.

Whirling around, the man raised a blaster gun. The hall lit up as he fired shots into the darkness. He allowed himself to catch his breath. Nothing there. He was safe – for now.

The disguise was slowing him down. He reached up and tore off his face. It came away easily, revealing the man to be an undercover DNAlien – a henchman of the evil HighBreed.

A laser blast scorched the air by his deformed head. The alien was off and running at once, ducking and weaving through the shadows, frantically trying to avoid his pursuer. As he ran, he twisted and took aim with his gun. But before he could pull the trigger, he slipped on a patch of spilled oil

The alien slid across the floor. He struggled to stay upright, but it was a losing battle. He quickly lost his balance and came crashing to the ground. The gun slipped from his fingers and clattered noisily across the floor.

The alien scuttled forwards, its claw-like

hands scrabbling for the weapon. Just as he reached it, another energy blast tore through the air. The gun exploded in a shower of bright blue sparks.

The DNAlien leaped back to his feet. His single bulging eye scanned the shadows. Nothing moved. Whoever was chasing him had ducked back out of sight. Wasting no time, the alien turned on his heels and darted off in search of a way out.

The inside of the plant was a maze of narrow, winding passageways. Losing his pursuer shouldn't be too difficult. All he had to do was keep his wits about him and not run into a . . . trap?

The alien stumbled to a stop. Up ahead, two red lights blinked into life. He watched them grow steadily brighter, then realised – too late – what they were. A large van was reversing directly towards him!

Before the DNAlien could run again, two bands of purple energy wrapped around his arms, handcuffing him. He writhed and wrestled against the bonds, as they slowly pulled him towards the back of the van.

When the alien was almost at the vehicle, the rear door slid upwards. The creature squealed and struggled when he spotted what was waiting for him inside the van: a Null Void Projector.

With a final, deafening scream, the alien creature was dragged into the van and sucked into the dark, empty, endless wasteland of the Null Void.

The scream was still hanging in the air when two figures emerged from inside the vehicle. The larger of the two curled all four of his arms, flexing his powerful muscles. The four-armed alien looked down at his partner, and grinned. 'Another one bites the dust!'

The van rattled along a city street, its headlights shining like beacons in the evening gloom. The larger alien was behind the wheel. He was from a race known as the Tetramands. Many years ago, Ben had been able to use the Omnitrix to transform into an alien just like him – the super-strong Four Arms.

'Hey, Helen. Did you see the look on that DNAlien's face when we roped him?' the big alien laughed. 'That was one freaked out . . .' He noticed his partner wasn't laughing along with him. 'What?'

In the passenger seat, Helen was gazing out of the window. She was also an alien – a member of the lightning-fast Kinceleran race. Kinceleran DNA was also stored in the Omnitrix, allowing Ben to transform into the alien he called XLR8 a few years back.

'Forget it, Manny,' said Helen, briefly glancing in her partner's direction.

Manny began to prod her with one of his free arms. 'Helen, come on. Talk to me.'

'Quit it!' Helen snapped.

'Come on.'

'Stop. I said no,' Helen said, slapping his hand away.

'Ow!' Manny yelped. 'What is with you?'

'Nothing's with me. I just . . .' Helen turned back to the window and gazed into the dark. 'I wish Pierce were here.'

'Yeah, I know,' Manny nodded. 'Me too.'

'Yeah, right.'

'What do you mean?' asked Manny. 'Your brother and me – '

'Argued over every single mission,' said Helen, cutting him off. She pulled a face and began to imitate Manny and Pierce's voices. 'Who's in charge? Do it this way. No, my plan's much better.'

Manny hesitated. 'OK, yeah. We disagreed. But now that he's . . .' He cut the sentence short when he saw the sadness in Helen's eyes. 'Helen, I'm just trying to do what we all agreed to do,' he said, softly. 'Fry every DNAlien we can find.'

A piercing alarm rang out from the van's dashboard and a display screen lit up. A trio of red dots flashed in the middle of the monitor.

'Three of them, and they're close,' said Helen, quickly.

'Where?'

Helen studied the display. 'Back at the sewerage plant.'

SCREEEEEECH!

Manny wrenched the wheel and pulled up the handbrake, sending the van into a sharp turn. He gritted his teeth and slammed his foot down on the accelerator pedal. The tyres squealed on the tarmac, as the vehicle roared back towards the sewerage plant.

Back at the plant, Helen and Manny were searching the grounds. A high-tech, alien-looking gadget in Manny's hand flashed wildly.

'Can't get a lock on them,' he muttered. 'Stupid machine.'

'Want me to try?' Helen offered.

'No,' Manny hissed. 'Sssh!'

Slowly, he waved the machine around, left to right, scanning for the aliens. At last, the outline of three figures appeared on the built-in display screen. Manny adjusted the controls and voices began to crackle over the gadget's speaker system.

'Are you sure you know what you're doing, Sherlock?' asked the first voice. It was male, probably around seventeen years old.

'For once can you keep your mouth shut and open your eyes? Just follow the blueprints,' sighed a second voice. This one was also male, but it sounded a couple of years younger than the first.

'Would you both be quiet?' said a female voice. 'It could be a guard or something.'

'I'd swear the alien ran into here,' said the first voice.

'Well,' replied the girl, 'there's no sign of him now.'

On his screen, Manny saw the older boy bend down and pick something up off the ground. 'Oo-hoo-hoo,' said the boy, 'come and check this out.'

A hiss of static burst from the speaker on Manny's scanner, making it impossible to hear what the boy said next.

'What did he say?' frowned Helen.

'Doesn't matter,' Manny replied, slipping the scanner back on to his belt. He clenched all four of his powerful fists and cracked his knuckles, noisily. 'Let's dust 'em!'

CHAPTER TWO

TRACKING THEIR PREY

Helen caught Manny by one of his arms. 'We can't. The Eradicannon needs more time to re-charge.' She glanced over to the van. 'How about we follow them instead? Maybe they'll lead us to a whole nest of DNAliens.'

She turned back to her partner, but he was already on the move, scaling a building to get a better shot at his prey.

'Manny,' she sighed, setting off after him.

With a grunt, Manny pulled himself up on to the roof. He darted to the edge and peered down. The three aliens were there. They were in human disguises, and standing beside a green car.

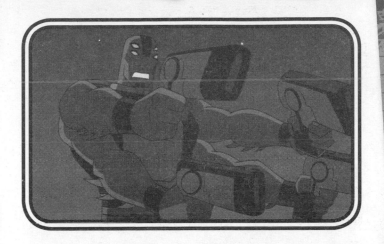

Reaching into the holsters on his belt, Manny drew four laser pistols and took aim. He held his breath, lining each shot up perfectly.

A blur of speed shot across the roof. Helen stopped directly in front of him, preventing him from taking the shot. In a flash, she stripped him of the weapons.

'You just novor liston to mc, do you?' Helen scowled.

Down on the ground, the three figures were climbing into the car. Manny watched with dismay as the engine began to roar.

'They're getting away!' he complained.

'No,' said Helen, extending her wrist. 'They aren't.'

SHNINK!

A round green locator tool shot from a gadget on Helen's arm. It spun through the air like a flying disk. Just before the car pulled away, the locator disk attached itself to the rear bumper. Now, no matter where the three aliens might go, Helen and Manny would be able to track and follow them.

Later, back at their headquarters, Helen was sitting alone. She was watching the monitor of a hand-held video player. On screen, her brother, Pierce, was speaking directly into the camera.

'August tenth,' he said. 'We zapped another DNAlien. Third one this month. Only . . .' Pierce hesitated and glanced down at the ground. 'Something weird happened. We had the creep cornered. I got my energy lash wrapped around him, but just before Manny hooked 'em, he flashed a Plumber's badge.

'Figured it had to be fake, but now I don't know. What if it was real? What if we were wrong about – '

A door opening on the roof behind him cut him off. On screen, Pierce turned to see

Helen emerge from the door, with Manny right behind her.

'Helen, what is with you?' Manny asked her. 'Every night you're up here.'

'Sometimes I like to look at the stars,' Helen explained. 'You know, think about what's out there.'

'Out there?' Manny spluttered. 'Out there is why we're all contaminated freaks. It's why we're kicking alien butt so nobody has to go through what happened to us.'

Pierce gave a sigh and walked over to join the others. 'Would you two stop it?' he shouted. 'Every day it's the same fight. I can't babysit you forever, you know?'

The picture on screen froze as the recording came to an end. Helen touched the on-screen picture of her brother. 'I know,' she whispered.

The door to the room slid open and
Helen looked up. Manny stood in the doorway,
beckoning to her. 'Come here,' he said. 'I wanna
show you something.'

She hopped down from her chair and
followed him through to another room. Monitors
and complicated alien machinery covered all
the walls.

'I fed the thermo scans from the
sewerage plant into one of Pierce's computers,'
Manny explained. He pushed a few buttons and
looked up at the largest of the display screens.

Absolutely nothing appeared to happen.

'Wow,' said Helen, sarcastically. 'Great. I am so impressed.'

'Stupid machine,' growled Manny, thumping a fist down on to the control console. The screen flickered for a moment, and then the silhouettes of the three figures they'd seen at the plant appeared.

Static flashed across the monitor for a few seconds, and then the outlines were replaced by images of three humans. Helen and Manny didn't know it, but the humans were Ben Tennyson, his cousin Gwen, and their friend, Kevin E. Levin.

'Those are aliens?' frowned Helen. 'They look human.'

'They must be wearing disguises. I would've caught them if you hadn't gone and stopped me.'

'They outnumbered us,' Helen reminded him. 'I stopped you from starting a fight that we would never have been able to win.'

'Well, Pierce would definitely have done it,' Manny snapped.

Helen spun around to face him. Anger burned in the green centres of her eyes. 'No, he wouldn't. And don't you dare use him as an excuse! Pierce found all this alien junk and made it work. Pierce brought us together. And when Pierce was in charge, we were careful. The one time we weren't . . .' Her voice broke off as tears began to roll down her cheeks.

Manny sighed. 'I'm sorry, OK? Look, tomorrow we'll track their signal. We'll take it slow. We'll be careful. Just the way Pierce was.'

Helen nodded her head once, then walked out of the lab, wiping the tears from her eyes. Manny watched her go, then turned back to the monitor.

'But once we find them,' he said to himself, 'then we'll handle things my way.'

The next night, Kevin's car weaved through the late-evening traffic. None of the three occupants of the vehicle had even noticed the van following a hundred metres or so behind them.

Inside the van, Helen fiddled with the controls of the hand-held scanner.

'What are they doing?' asked Manny

from the driver's seat.

'I can't lock in on them, but it sounds like they're arguing.' Helen glanced across at her partner. 'Do you think they know that we're tailing them?'

A grin spread across Manny's face. 'Why don't we make sure?'

Up ahead, the car was pulling into a petrol station. Manny wound down his window and thrust an arm out. Helen realised he was holding a blaster gun.

'Manny, no!' she cried, but her partner didn't listen. Manny squeezed the trigger, sending bright bolts of blue energy screaming along the street.

Before the blasts could hit the car, a large petrol tanker pulled out behind it. The laser bolts hit the wheels of the truck, sending it into a spin. The back end of the tanker swung wide, tearing through the petrol station and smashing one of the pumps.

The front end of the truck crashed hard into an oncoming car. Flames began to flicker across the engine bay and into the driver's cab.

Leaping from Kevin's car, Ben spotted the shattered fuel pump. Petrol was quickly flooding out, forming an expanding puddle over the forecourt.

'If that tanker goes up, we're talking about a major bonfire,' he said.

Kevin jumped from the car and began sprinting towards the front of the truck. 'I'll get the driver,' he cried.

'And I've got the truck,' nodded Ben. 'Gwen, give us cover.'

'I'm on it,' Gwen told him, clambering from the back seat of the car. The two of them ran towards the back of the tanker, neither one noticing the van screeching to a halt a few metres behind them.

'I can't believe you did that!' Helen yelled at Manny.

'So what?' scowled Manny. 'They're getting away.'

By the time Manny unclipped his seatbelt, Helen had already left the van.

A crowd of spectators had gathered near the truck. They watched on, frightened, but desperate to see what was going to happen next. Gwen had some bad news for them. She blasted the ground in front of the onlookers with her energy powers. The tarmac road cracked and curved upwards, forming a solid wall in front of the flaming truck.

Meanwhile, Kevin had almost reached the driver's cab. As he ran, he brushed his fingers against the side of the steel tanker, absorbing its strength. By the time he reached the door of the cab, his body was covered entirely in living metal.

'How come I always get the easy jobs?' he wondered, as he tore the door off its hinges.

He pulled the unconscious driver from his seat and hoisted him over his shoulder. Petrol flooded around his feet and Kevin started to run. Sparks rained down from the burning cab. Kevin pushed himself to move even faster, but it was too late.

WHOOSH!

Kevin heard the petrol catch light. Even in his powerful metal form he could feel the burning heat of the huge fireball as it raced up behind him, the flames getting ever closer.

CHAPTER THREE

TEAM-MATE TROUBLES

The flames licked at Kevin's back. He knew the fire couldn't hurt him in his current form, but the driver would be burned to a crisp. There was only one chance. He had to try something he'd never attempted before.

Throwing himself into a forward roll, Kevin reached out with one hand and touched the hard concrete ground. With his other hand he took hold of the unconscious truck driver's bare arm.

Kevin's shiny metallic surface gave way to rough, grey stone. He almost cheered with relief when he saw that the driver, too, was becoming covered in a tough concrete exterior. The flames engulfed them as the fire tore across the forecourt towards the broken petrol pump, but the stone saved them both from being hurt.

Once the inferno had rushed harmlessly past them, Kevin stood up and nodded to Ben. 'Your turn,' he said.

Ben didn't waste any time in activating the Omnitrix. The familiar swirl of green energy wrapped around him, transforming him into the moth-like Big Chill.

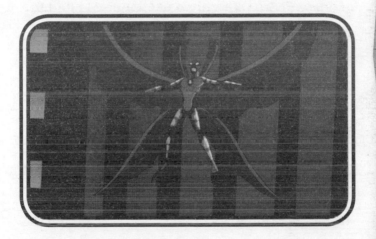

A short distance away, Helen watched in amazement as Big Chill flew over the burning petrol station, breathing freezing fog down over the flames. As the frozen air hit the forecourt, the fire was snuffed out. In just a few seconds, the whole petrol station was encased in ice.

Kevin set the truck driver down on the ground. Using his powers, he returned him back to normal. All traces of the stone that had saved the driver from the fire quickly disappeared.

'Hey, you!' bellowed a voice.

Kevin looked up to see Manny standing in the middle of the street. He had Kevin's car held above his head, and a wicked glint in all four of his eyes.

'Catch!' Manny cried. He hurled the car with all his strength.

Kevin's eyes went wide as he saw his car hurtling through the air towards him. 'Not my ride!' he groaned.

SLAM!

The front of the car hit Kevin in the chest. It knocked him off his feet and smashed him into the side of the now frozen truck.

'Kevin!' cried Gwen, who had seen the whole thing. She hurried over to help him, but before she could get there, something began to circle around her at tremendous speed. Faster and faster it went, until Gwen was standing in the centre of a whirling tornado.

The wind whipped her into the air, sending her flipping end over end, around and around, until she didn't know which way was up. Then, just as suddenly as it had started, the tornado stopped. Gwen screamed as she realised she was plunging head-first towards the ground.

Big Chill spun around at the sound of his cousin's cry. Taking a deep breath, he blasted out a stream of frosty air. An ice-slide formed below Gwen just in time, and she slid down to a safe, but chilly, landing.

Over by the petrol tanker, Kevin wasn't so lucky. A hulking fist slammed him hard against the ground, shattering the concrete. As Kevin slumped unconscious, his rock-hard protective coating vanished, leaving him completely at Manny's mercy.

The four-armed alien lifted Kevin by the back of the neck and studied him as if he were an insect. He barely noticed Helen rushing over to join him.

'You see that?' she asked. 'They saved that guy.'

'Who cares?' Manny shrugged. 'One of them's hurt. Now's our chance to take them.'

'No way,' said Helen, glancing over to where Big Chill was transforming back into Ben.

'Not until we talk.'

In a heartbeat she zoomed away, leaving Manny to drag Kevin over to the van.

Gwen was shivering as Ben helped her back to her feet. Neither of them noticed the van driving past them, or could have guessed what was inside.

'W-where's K-Kevin,' said Gwen through chattering teeth.

Ben sighed heavily and stared off into the night. 'Gone,' he said.

Back at his house, Ben was on the warpath. He paced the floor of his bedroom, ranting furiously.

'And what really bugs me is one of them was an XLR8,' he complained. 'I mean, I used to turn into that species. None of it makes any sense.' He looked across to Gwen, who was sitting quietly on the bed. 'Gwen? Jump in at any time.'

'Ssh,' Gwen hissed. 'I'm concentrating.'

Ben frowned. 'On what?'

'I'm at one with the cosmic mana, feeling the energy of the Universe flowing around and through me,' Gwen replied, casually. She had her eyes closed. When she opened them, they glowed with mystical energy.

'Groovy,' Ben replied. 'Why?'

'So that I can locate Kevin. Which I have.' The pink glow faded and her eyes returned to normal. She jumped up off the bed. 'Now all we have to do is rescue him.'

'Oh,' Ben scowled. 'Is that all?'

A bright yellow ball of energy floated above the floor of Manny and Helen's headquarters. Inside lay Kevin – trapped and helpless, but wide awake. Like Ben, Manny was pacing the floor.

'What were you thinking?' he yelled at Helen. 'We had them on the ropes. We could've nailed three monsters at once!'

'Monsters?' snorted Kevin. 'That's a laugh coming from a Halloween reject like you!'

Manny flexed his muscles and narrowed his eyes. 'Sounds like the alien dirt bag is asking for another fight.'

'Let me out of this bubble,' growled Kevin. 'Then we'll see what you've got.'

'Quiet,' snapped Helen. The tone of her voice took them both by surprise. 'You sound like a couple of young children fighting in the school playground.'

'I'm not anything like him,' said Kevin and Manny at the same time.

Furious, Manny stormed over to the bubble and pushed a hand through it. His powerful fingers wrapped around Kevin's face and began to pull. Kevin hissed with pain.

'Manny, stop that. It's not a mask,' Helen cried out. 'You're hurting him!'

'That's my face,' snarled Kevin, pulling free of Manny's grip.

'It doesn't matter,' Manny bellowed. 'He's an alien, and I say we feed him to the Eradicannon.'

Kevin patted his face, making sure it was still intact. 'The . . . uh . . . Eradi-what?'

Manny gestured towards a nearby alien gadget. 'A disintegrator beam. It turns scum like you into dust.'

'That's not a disintegrator, you dufus!' Kevin laughed. 'It's a Null Void Projector.'

Manny frowned. 'A Null Void . . . what?'

'Probably a Mark One,' continued Kevin, looking more closely at the device. 'It's a museum piece. And you are a pinhead.'

Drawing his guns, Manny blasted the energy bubble. Inside, Kevin cried out in pain as he was thrown violently around. His head slammed hard against the wall of the prison, and he slumped down into an unconscious heap in the bubble.

'Why did you do that?' gasped Helen.

'He was getting on my nerves.'

'What if you're wrong, Manny?' Helen asked. 'What if he's not an alien?'

'You saw his powers, he's gotta be an alien,' replied Manny. He picked up a hand-held device from a tabletop. 'I'll prove it to you.'

The gadget bleeped as Manny switched it on. A list of alien races appeared on the device's screen. He scrolled through them, trying to find a match.

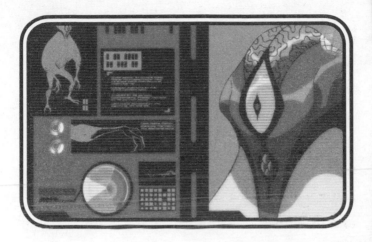

'Gotta be one like him in here,' he said, flicking through dozens of different aliens.

'Manny, listen to me,' Helen pleaded. 'That guy in there, whatever he is, has a Plumber's badge.'

'So?'

'There was something in Pierce's diary. One of the aliens we nailed last summer – he had one, too.'

'Big deal,' Manny shrugged. 'If he has a badge, it's a fake. Him and his pals, they're all alien villains.'

'Then why would they save that driver? Why did they stop the truck from exploding?'

'I don't know and I don't care. They're all aliens,' he nodded towards the Null Void Projector. 'And you know exactly what we do with aliens.'

CHAPTER FOUR

FIVE WAY FIGHT

A few miles across town from Helen and Manny's base, an overcrowded bus slowly chugged its way along a busy street. On the back seats, Ben and Gwen waited impatiently for the driver to speed up.

'What kind of heroes take the bus?' Gwen muttered.

'Neither of us is old enough to drive. What do you want me to do?' asked Ben. He held his hand to his ear, as if he were talking on the telephone. 'Hi, Mum. We have to go fight some aliens. Can you give us a ride?'

Gwen shook her head. 'OK, whatever. I'm just worried, that's all.'

'About Kevin?'

'Well, yeah, what else? We need to find

him before . . . You know. Before something bad happens.' She smiled, bashfully. 'Not that I care or anything. I mean, come on – how could anyone care about a person who's that rude and unreliable, and . . . and annoying? It's ridiculous.' She gave her cousin a slap on the arm. 'How could you even think of saying something like that?'

'Actually,' Ben coughed, 'I didn't say anything at all.'

Gwen felt her cheeks go red. She turned and looked out at the buildings creeping by outside. Why couldn't this thing go any faster?

Helen studied the screen of the alien tracker. The shape of the bus was outlined on the display in red.

'Aliens,' she announced. 'And they are

headed this way. We need to get ready.'

Manny picked up a blaster pistol and the energy snare weapon he had used to capture the DNAlien at the sewerage plant. Helen zipped speedily around the lab, picking up her own weapons.

'OK,' nodded Manny, when they were both ready. 'Let's go!'

A minute or so later, the alien-hunters stepped through the front door of their headquarters and out into the cool evening air.

'How close are they?' Manny asked.

'Very,' replied a voice, before Helen had even opened her mouth.

Manny and Helen turned to see Ben and Gwen standing nearby. Pink energy crackled between Gwen's fingertips. 'Now,' she said, 'give us back our friend.'

Ben raised an eyebrow. 'Friend?'

Gwen blushed again. 'Team-mate, co-worker, whatever. Could we not talk about this at some other time?'

'Hey,' Ben protested, 'I'm not the one who always – '

Helen fired an energy blast at the wall above the heroes. Rubble rained down on Ben, knocking him to the ground. He lay there, eyes closed, groaning in pain.

Gwen bent down to help him, but not before she unleashed an attack of her own. Her power beam hit Manny directly in the chest, sending him stumbling backwards. The battle had begun!

Inside his bubble prison, Kevin was waking up. He groaned as he heard the screeches of the laser weapons outside.

'Sounds like my rescuers need rescuing,' he said. From his pocket, he pulled out a few coins. Concentrating, he absorbed their properties. They barely contained enough metal for him to cover his hand in a dull copper coating. 'Huh,' he muttered. 'I guess this will have to do.'

Summoning all his strength, Kevin drove a punch down, hard, against the floor of the bubble. Pain shot through him, burning like fire across his body. Still he pushed, until he felt his fingers emerge through the bottom of the weird energy prison.

Just . . . a little . . . more, he thought, forcing his arm further through the wall of the bubble. With a triumphant yell, he found what he was looking for. His metallic fingers wrapped around the prison projector, and squeezed. As the device shattered, the bubble disappeared with a **POP**.

'Huh,' he smiled, getting his breath back. 'The four-armed freak is not the only tough guy around.'

He crossed to the wall and touched one of the solid iron pipes that ran from floor to ceiling. The pain in his arm faded as his whole body took on the dull sheen of the metal. Kevin smiled, grimly. It was time for him to get his own back.

Outside, Gwen had dragged the still-unconscious Ben behind a low wall. Energy blasts rained down around them, pinning them in place.

'Come on, Ben,' she pleaded. 'I need a little help here.'

Manny and Helen stopped firing as the wall behind them exploded outwards. A metal figure emerged, his face a mask of anger.

'Nothing like a little iron in your diet to perk you right up,' Kevin growled, setting his sights on Manny.

The four-armed alien launched himself at Kevin, his enormous fists raised.

'Manny, wait!' Helen cried, but her partner was no longer listening to her. His first punch caught Kevin on the side of the head, sending him spinning on to the pavement.

Kevin recovered quickly. He caught Manny's next punch and twisted the alien's arm. A metal elbow slammed into Manny's cheek, making him cry out in shock. He didn't notice Kevin's uppercut until it hit against the bottom of his jaw.

Staggering backwards, Manny shook the cobwebs from his head. He tensed his bulging muscles. If it was a fight this guy wanted, it was a fight he would get!

Meanwhile, Helen was doing her best to keep Gwen and Ben trapped behind the wall. She squeezed the trigger of her blaster gun.

BLAM, BLAM, BLAM!

A power beam streaked towards her, but Helen was too fast. She dodged sideways and continued her attack.

'Stand still, will you?' growled Gwen, unleashing more energy bolts.

Down on the ground, Ben opened his eyes. His head ached badly. He groaned, rubbing a bump on the back of his skull. 'I've got to start wearing a helmet.'

Groggily, Ben pulled himself up and squinted down at the Omnitrix. Like everything else at the moment, it looked blurry and indistinct. Ben flicked through the aliens, not noticing that he was staggering out into the middle of the battlefield.

'Ben!' cried Gwen. She moved to catch her cousin, but a sudden volley of laser blasts held her back.

'OK, which one?' drawled Ben, still going through his selection of alien forms. 'Eenie, meenie – '

'Get out of the way!' cried Kevin to Ben, slamming Manny against a wall. Huge chunks of rock broke away from the building and crashed to the ground just centimetres from Ben's feet.

Manny managed to unclip a remote

control from his belt and stabbed his fingers against the buttons. His van suddenly came roaring backwards around the corner. As it drew closer, the rear door slid open, revealing that the Null Void Projector had been activated.

Distracted, Gwen turned at the sound of the van's engine. Seizing her chance, Helen whizzed round the girl a few hundred times in the space of a second. Gwen spun round and round on the spot, then fell forwards on to the cold, hard pavement.

Kevin raced over to Gwen as fast as he could, shouting her name. She seemed to be all right, and he knelt beside her, cradling her head. But he was unaware that Manny and Helen were closing in.

'Now,' growled the four-armed alien, activating his energy snare. 'Let's finish 'em!

A band of purple alien energy snaked out from the snare and wrapped around Ben's wrist. A second snare caught his other arm. Ben kicked and struggled, but it was no use. Without the use of his hands he couldn't reach the Omnitrix, and in human form he was nowhere near strong enough to break free of the energy bonds that trapped him.

With a yank, he was lifted off the ground. He felt the Projector pulling him, dragging him in. He was totally helpless. He saw Kevin move to catch him, but by then it was too late.

With a lingering scream of terror, Ben was sucked into the van and dragged into the swirling vortex of the Null Void.

CHAPTER FIVE

INTO THE NULL VOID

Gwen and Kevin stared into the swirling heart of the Null Void Projector, too shocked to move. Had it really happened? Was Ben really gone?

'Well, it may be a museum piece, but it did the job on your friend,' crowed Manny. He and Helen had their guns trained on the two heroes. 'And you two are next.'

A faint sound from the Null Void Projector suddenly caught everyone's attention. They all turned in time to see a green hand stretch out from inside the swirling portal. The hand gripped the edge of the machine and began to pull.

The red and yellow head of Swampfire emerged from inside the machine. Amazingly, Ben had managed to activate the Omnitrix in there! With a heave, the alien hero dragged himself free of the Null Void.

Kevin nodded, impressed. 'I taught him that,' he boasted.

'No you didn't,' Gwen replied.

Swampfire drew himself up to his full height and began to advance on the aliens Manny and Helen.

'It's not a disintegrator,' Helen gasped.

Manny didn't care. He took aim with his blasters. 'Lousy stinking – ' The screech of his laser blasts drowned out the rest of the insult. The energy bolts punched holes straight through Swampfire's chest. The alien hero didn't even flinch.

When Manny stopped shooting, the holes in Swampfire's body healed themselves at once. Swampfire grinned. Now it was his turn.

Throwing out his hands, Swampfire unleashed a jet of blisteringly hot flames straight at Manny. The four-armed alien staggered backwards under the heat. He tried to fight back, but Swampfire's blasts were too powerful. With a groan, Manny buckled and collapsed to the ground.

Swampfire turned to face the startled Helen. 'Now,' he boomed, 'put down your weapons and just listen for five minutes, OK?'

Helen hesitated, then slowly set her gun and energy snare down on the pavement. 'All ears,' she said.

Half an hour later, Ben, Gwen and Kevin stood together. Helen and Manny stood beside them, still trying to understand everything they had just been told.

'So, we're all aliens?' asked Helen.

'Kinda,' shrugged Ben. 'One of your

parents must've been human. The other – well, not so much.'

'Yeah?' demanded Manny, fiercely. 'Then how come you can switch back but we can't?'

Ben shrugged again. 'Luck of the draw.'

'But look at it this way,' smirked Kevin, staring up at Manny, 'your human version is probably even uglier.'

Manny clenched his fists. 'You wanna go another round?' he growled.

'Any time, pal.'

'Tell your boyfriend to back off,' Helen told Gwen.

'No, tell yours to . . .' Gwen began, before she realised what had been said. 'What? He's not my boyfriend!'

'Well you sure act like it,' said Helen.

'Don't tell me who my boyfriend isn't,' Gwen spluttered. She shook her head and quickly corrected herself. 'Is.'

'Think you're funny?' snarled Manny, prodding Kevin in the chest.

'Hey, you're the comedian. At least, you've got the face for it,' retorted Kevin.

Manny's breath hissed through his teeth. 'Boy, are you asking for it!'

'I'm begging for it,' said Kevin, raising his fists. 'Who's gonna give it to me?'

'I will, with three of my hands tied behind my back!'

'Hey, stop it. All of you,' cried Ben. He held up his hands. 'What am I? Your babysitter?'

Helen stopped arguing with Gwen and turned to look at Ben. 'You sound just like my brother,' she said. Sadness flashed across her face. 'Pierce was the one who always kept us grounded. The one who . . .'

She streaked away. In a heartbeat she was back, holding the hand-held video player. She held it up for the others to see. 'This is what he was talking about,' she said, switching the device on. They all stood in silence, watching Pierce talk about the alien who had been carrying the Plumber's badge.

'Don't you see, Manny?' Helen asked, when the video was done. 'We've been catching all those other aliens.'

'What other aliens?' frowned Ben.

Helen flicked a switch on the video gadget. Images of some of the aliens they had captured flashed up.

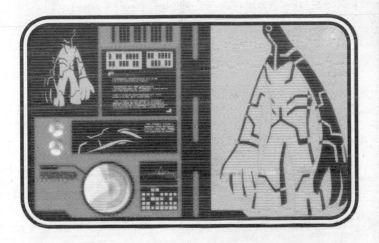

'Some of these might be other Plumber's kids,' Ben told them. 'Like us. Like you.'

'OK,' said Helen, decisively. 'In that case,

we have to go into that . . . Uh, what was it you called it?'

'Null Void,' said Kevin.

'Null Void. Round up everyone we captured and free all the ones who shouldn't be in there.'

Manny snorted. 'Not a chance.'

Helen turned to face him. 'Well, Manny, I'm doing it. Whether you come with me or not.'

'What? Why?'

'Because it's what Pierce would do.'

Manny glanced over at the Null Void Projector, then back to Helen. 'All right,' he nodded. 'For Pierce.'

Helen smiled and turned to face the others. 'Thanks,' she said. 'And sorry about . . .'

'Apology accepted,' said Kevin.

'Be careful,' Gwen told them.

'And good luck,' added Ben.

Manny and Helen approached the back of the van. The swirling red of the portal flared brightly around them, and in a flash they vanished into the Null Void.

Kevin shook his head. 'That is so not gonna go well,' he said.

'I dunno,' said Ben, disagreeing. 'On paper we don't look like such a good team.'

'There is that,' Kevin admitted. He turned away. 'Now, if you'll excuse me, I'm gonna go swipe some of their equipment.'

'Kevin!' Gwen scolded.

'So not cool, man,' said Ben. He shook his head. Kevin might be one of the good guys now, but it seemed that some habits were harder than others to break!

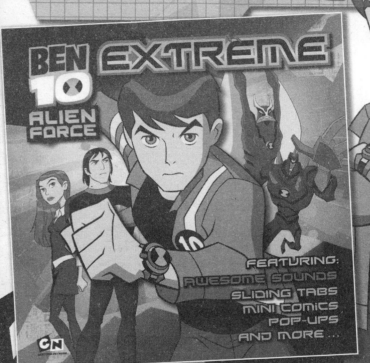